398.2　　Forest, Heather
FO
　　　　The baker's dozen

$13.95

cl

DATE			
DE 0 7 05			

© THE BAKER & TAYLOR CO.

THE BAKER'S DOZEN

A Colonial American Tale

Retold by

HEATHER FOREST

Illustrated by

SUSAN GABER

GULLIVER BOOKS

HARCOURT BRACE JOVANOVICH

San Diego   Austin   Orlando

Library of Congress Cataloging-in-Publication Data

Forest, Heather.

The baker's dozen: a colonial American tale/retold

by Heather Forest; illustrated by Susan Gaber. — 1st ed.

p.   cm.

"Gulliver books."

Summary: A greedy baker who offends a mysterious old woman

suffers misfortune in his business, until he discovers

what happens when generosity replaces greed.

ISBN 0-15-200412-2

[1. Folklore — United States.] I. Gaber, Susan, ill. II. Title.

PZ8.1.F76Bak 1988

398.2'7'0973 — dc19

[E]   87-17103

First edition

A   B   C   D   E

HBJ

The full-color artwork in this book was done on 90-lb. Fabriano cold press

100% cotton watercolor paper using watercolor and colored pencil.

The display and text type was set via the Linotron 202 in Baskerville.

Composition by Thompson Type, San Diego, California

Printed and bound by Tien Wah Press, Singapore

Production supervision by Warren Wallerstein and Eileen McGlone

Designed by Camilla Filancia

This book is dedicated to
the extra measure.

Van Amsterdam was a baker of great renown. People traveled for miles to buy his goods in Albanytown. He baked breads and cakes and muffins of every conceivable kind. He even invented a pastry of his very own design.

One day, just before the Winter Holidays, as Van Amsterdam was rolling out his cookie dough, he was inspired to cut out the shape of a jolly round man. Then he gave it two raisins for eyes and a little walnut for a mouth. After baking the cookie character, he painted it with red and white icing, so that it looked just like St. Nicholas.

He proudly put the cookie in his shop window. A passerby, noticing it, came in to order several. Delighted, Van Amsterdam spent the rest of the day cutting and baking those tasty cookies. Before long, the St. Nicholas cookie had become famous.

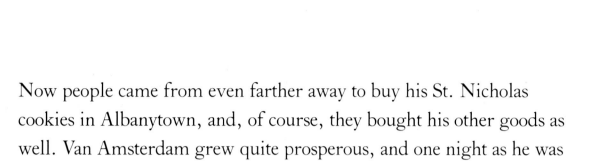

Now people came from even farther away to buy his St. Nicholas cookies in Albanytown, and, of course, they bought his other goods as well. Van Amsterdam grew quite prosperous, and one night as he was busy counting his money, a thought occurred to him. "If I use just a little less butter, no one will know. If I use just one less egg, they will scarcely be able to tell. If I use just a little less honey, then there will be more money for me!"

And no one did notice when Van Amsterdam started to use just a little less of all the fine ingredients he had always used in his baking. No one noticed, because Van Amsterdam was famous. People had stopped judging the quality of his goods, for his goods were famous, too.

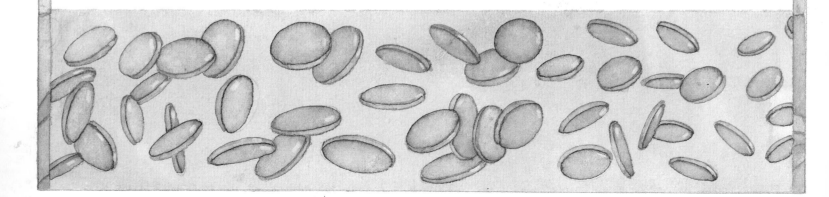

One day, into his shop came an old woman wearing a long black shawl over her head. She said, "Van Amsterdam, I have come to purchase one dozen of your famous St. Nicholas cookies."

"Very well," he said. Taking a cloth bag, he filled it with one dozen of his finest cookies and handed it to the old woman.

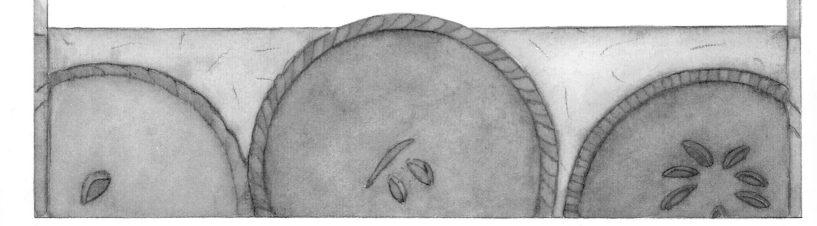

She took the bag from him, opened it, and then looked up, complaining, "Van Amsterdam, you've cheated me! I asked for a dozen cookies and, look here, you've given me only twelve."

"A dozen means twelve," Van Amsterdam stated firmly.

"A dozen means thirteen," she insisted, "and you're a greedy man!"

Van Amsterdam was a proud man who did not like
to be judged harshly by anyone. "I am a good
and honest baker!" he shouted. "A dozen means twelve
and not one more. How dare you call me greedy!
Get out of my store!"

As the old woman swept out of his shop,
she turned back and said,

"You'll be sorry, Van Amsterdam."

The next morning when Van Amsterdam took his loaves from the oven, he was shocked to discover that his bread tasted salty. His pies were sour. His cookies were so hard they couldn't be bitten. Everything he made turned out wrong. "I don't understand," he said. "Has it been so long since I used a proper measure that I have forgotten my recipes? Well, perhaps tomorrow will be better."

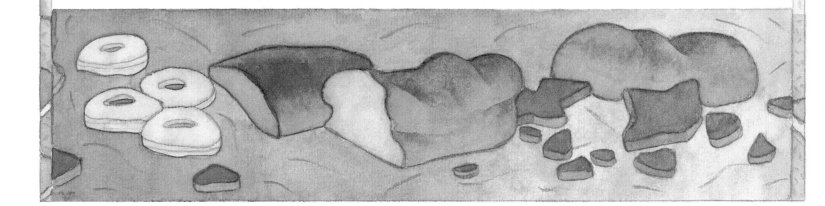

But it was no better. His breads rose so high he could not get them out of the oven. His cakes crumbled. Everything he baked tasted terrible.

It wasn't long before people who came to his shop to buy his pies and cakes and cookies and muffins had to admit that even though Van Amsterdam's Bakery was famous, the things he made there didn't taste good at all! So, they stopped coming. And as people stopped coming, Van Amsterdam stopped baking.

One day near Christmas, he sat in his shop with nothing left to sell but a small pile of those famous St. Nicholas cookies. He eyed his empty shelves and wondered, *Why has my fortune gone from so good to so bad?*

Van Amsterdam began to cry. It may have been the tears in his eyes, but it seemed to Van Amsterdam that the mouth on one of the St. Nicholas cookies was moving. He heard a voice say, "You'll never be rich because you're greedy."

At that moment there was a knock at the door, and into his shop came the old woman wearing the long black shawl. She said, "Van Amsterdam, I've come back to purchase one dozen of your famous St. Nicholas cookies."

Wide-eyed and trembling, Van Amsterdam reached for a bag and opened it. Into the bag he put twelve St. Nicholas cookies. He looked up at the old woman and then slowly put in one more. She took the bag from him with a grin. She opened it and carefully counted the cookies. "Thank you," she said.

Well, word went through the town that at
Van Amsterdam's shop a dozen means thirteen!
People started coming back to buy that baker's dozen.
Van Amsterdam began baking again, and he put an extra
measure into everything he made. Soon his shop prospered.

All the other bakers noticed how busy Van Amsterdam's shop had become, so they, too, began to give thirteen in a dozen.

The custom spread throughout the Colonies, for merchants had discovered that when generosity replaces greed, good fortune follows. And soon, in many a bakery store, a dozen meant twelve . . .

. . . and then one more.

Author's Note

In 1655, when Albany, New York, was still called Beverwyck,
there lived a colonial baker named Volckert Jan Pietersen
Van Amsterdam. This is the tale of how he came to give thirteen
in a dozen, inspiring an American custom that,
in some places, persists even today.